One Page Stories

By Doe Zantamata

www.happinessinyourlife.com

Special Thanks to:
Gary, Paul, Renate, Dennisse, Jill, Karen, Joel, Terry, Rhonda, and everyone, past and present, who has joined me on this life adventure and shared joy or taught me lessons that will last my whole life through.

ISBN-13: 978-1467945875
ISBN-10: 1467945870

This book is dedicated to all those who have
visited Happiness in Your Life on both
the website and social media pages.
It is because of you that this book exists.

It is also dedicated to you, dear reader.
It is because of you that the next one will exist!

Thank you, and Love to you,
Doe

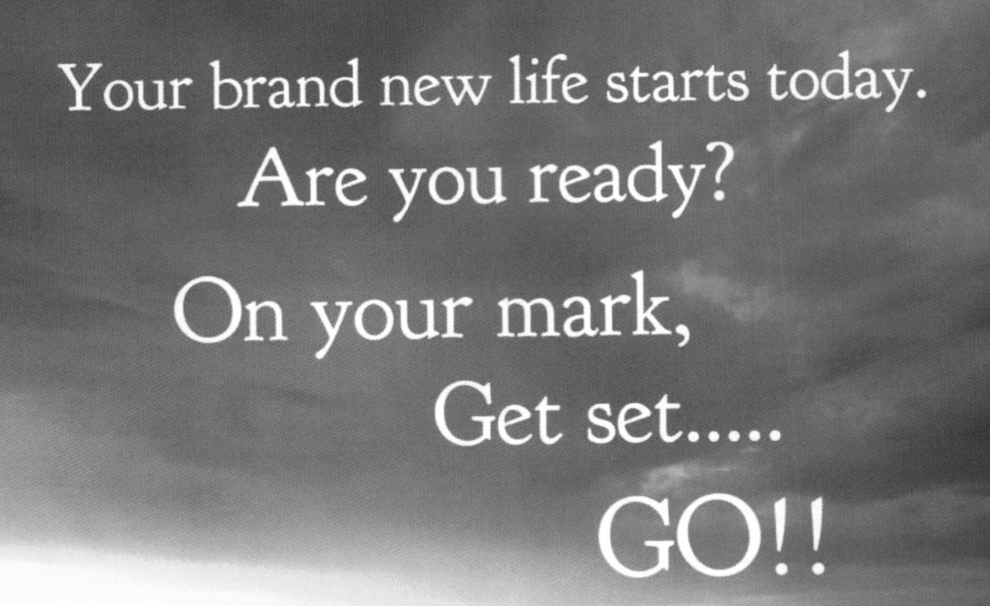
Your brand new life starts today.
Are you ready?
On your mark,
Get set.....
GO!!

START

The Story of You

One day, not long ago, a child was born.

That child was you.

The odds that you came into being were infinitesimally small. Your parents not only had to meet, but they had to be drawn together and remain together long enough for your creation to occur.

Whether they were madly in love for years, or only met once, you were definitely brought here on purpose.

The world has never seen a person quite like you in all of the millions of years it has existed, and no one exactly like you will ever exist again.

This is your time.

You will be here only a short while, less than a blink of an eye compared to the life of the world.

You will create, love, affect, learn, and share your life with many different people throughout your time here.

Some things in life to this point may seem to be struggles, or fruitless, and at times you may have felt as though things were just too hard. Those darkest moments in your life, the fact that you made it through each and every one of them, gave you proof that you are stronger and more determined that you ever thought you could be. Once you know and appreciate this, any limits you may have had disappear in an instant.

Those moments of joy you've shared in your life with others, they were all only possible because of you. Without you, they would have never been. Imagine each and every person with whom you've ever shared a laugh, a hug, or a kiss. If you were not here, in each of those moments, they would have been standing alone.

Because of you, there is more joy in the world. More hope, more compassion, and more optimism.

What you do in your lifetime may only seem like a tiny stone thrown into a lake, but you must always remember the ripple. Every thought, every word you speak, and every action you take ripples out to hundreds, if not thousands of people, many who you have never met. When you extend kindness, you inspire others to do the same. When you smile, you create another smile on the person who sees yours.

Those who are completely unaware see only darkness.

Those who have awakened, see light where others don't.

Those who are on their journey to enlightenment know that the light lives inside of them, and carry it wherever they go.

Thank you so very much for being here.

Polyanna

One brisk fall evening, Mary went to dinner with her friend Sue, and Sue brought another one of her friends along, Jeff. He seemed alright, except that he complained about the food, the service, that it was too loud, and that another family wasn't "controlling" their kids.

Mary said, "My dinner was great, it was really busy but I'm sure the staff were doing the best they could, the noise wasn't loud for how busy it was, and the kids seemed to be laughing a lot, but they were just having fun."

Jeff got annoyed, and snapped, "Mary, are you always such a Pollyanna?"

Mary didn't know what that meant, but Sue shot him a stern look, and quickly changed the subject.

Mary looked it up online when she got home.

From the dictionary: "pollyanna; a person characterized by irrepressible optimism and a tendancy to find the good in everything, an excessively or blindly optimistic person."

Mary exclaimed, "Wow! What a great compliment! I'll have to remember to thank him!"

You can never choose what people say or do, but you can always choose how you let it affect you.

Face the World

The one thing we never see our whole lives, is our face. Yet it's the one thing that people remember about us. They may not remember our name, or what type of ice cream we like, but they will always remember our face. If you close one eye and look down, you can see your nose and maybe a little more, that's it. The rest of the time, what you're seeing is not your face, but a reflection of it in a mirror, or photo of it.

Have you ever looked at a photo immediately after it was taken, then looked at it again several years later, only to see a totally different image of you than you remembered?

You may have felt "old" at the time, but looking back 7 or 8 years, you look at the same photo and think "I looked so young!"

The image did not change, but your perception of it did. Your view of the world, even of concrete images, literally changes the way you see things.

Whatever age you are, you are young. There are 97 year olds who wish they were as young as you! Appreciate yourself as you are today...EXACTLY as you are today.

Don't wait ten years to see the beauty of the young face which you currently wear. Also, make sure to give people a beautiful, smiling face to remember you by...because they certainly will!

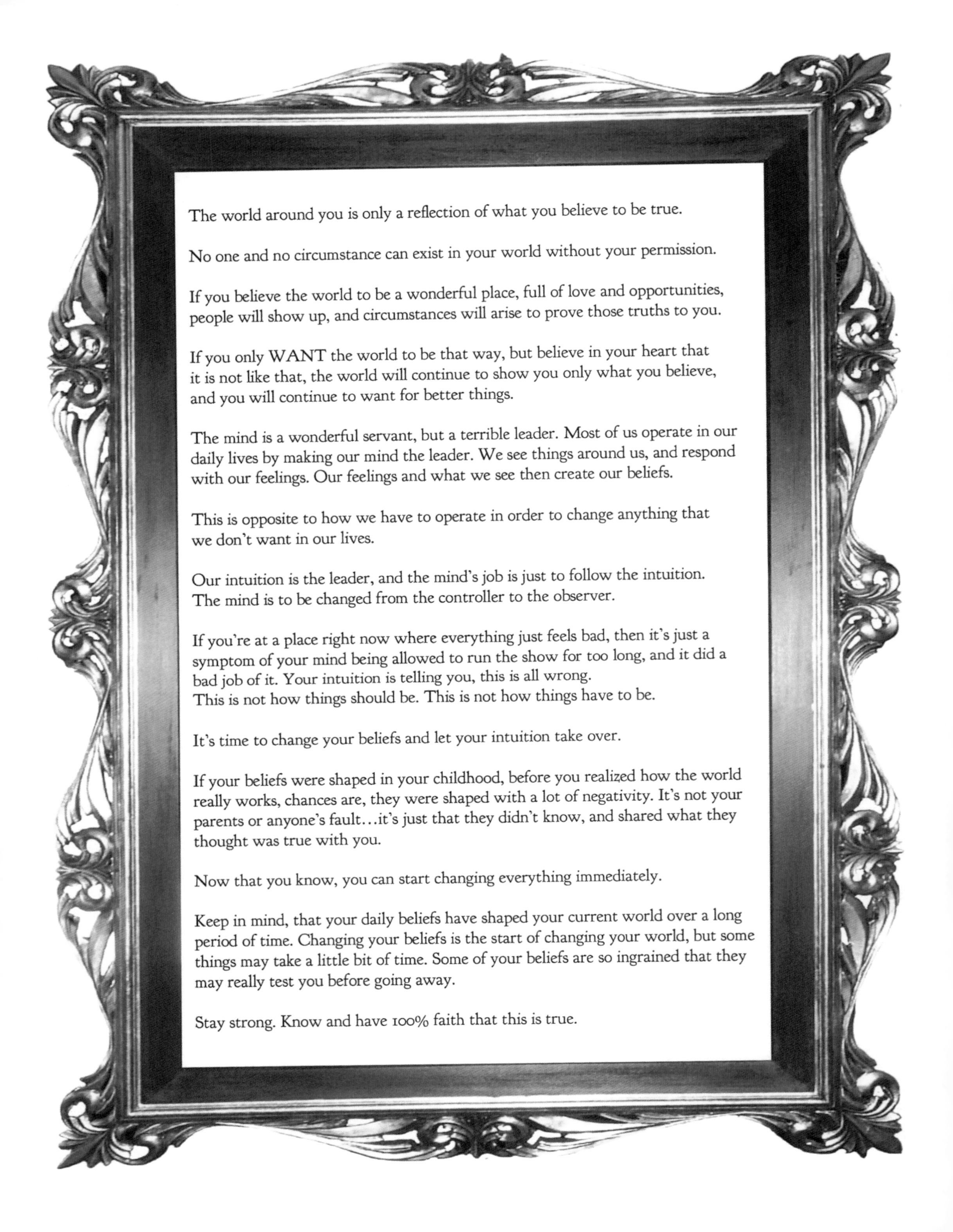

The world around you is only a reflection of what you believe to be true.

No one and no circumstance can exist in your world without your permission.

If you believe the world to be a wonderful place, full of love and opportunities, people will show up, and circumstances will arise to prove those truths to you.

If you only WANT the world to be that way, but believe in your heart that it is not like that, the world will continue to show you only what you believe, and you will continue to want for better things.

The mind is a wonderful servant, but a terrible leader. Most of us operate in our daily lives by making our mind the leader. We see things around us, and respond with our feelings. Our feelings and what we see then create our beliefs.

This is opposite to how we have to operate in order to change anything that we don't want in our lives.

Our intuition is the leader, and the mind's job is just to follow the intuition. The mind is to be changed from the controller to the observer.

If you're at a place right now where everything just feels bad, then it's just a symptom of your mind being allowed to run the show for too long, and it did a bad job of it. Your intuition is telling you, this is all wrong.
This is not how things should be. This is not how things have to be.

It's time to change your beliefs and let your intuition take over.

If your beliefs were shaped in your childhood, before you realized how the world really works, chances are, they were shaped with a lot of negativity. It's not your parents or anyone's fault…it's just that they didn't know, and shared what they thought was true with you.

Now that you know, you can start changing everything immediately.

Keep in mind, that your daily beliefs have shaped your current world over a long period of time. Changing your beliefs is the start of changing your world, but some things may take a little bit of time. Some of your beliefs are so ingrained that they may really test you before going away.

Stay strong. Know and have 100% faith that this is true.

The Habit of Thinking

Habits are changeable.

Try this…take your computer mouse and move it to somewhere else on your desk. Or, move the garbage can in your kitchen to a new place. You will be really surprised at how many times you go for the mouse in the old place even though you know it's not there anymore. You won't believe how many times you toss something or almost toss something in the place where the garbage can used to be. Eventually, though, the new places, or habits, will become more normal and familiar.

The same is true for super positive thinking. If you decide to really believe those super positive beliefs, it will still take a little while before they become habits. Once they are habits, they will just become the way you think, react, and operate in your daily life. This is when things will really start to change for the better.

Now, nobody admits to being a "pessimist." Nobody. Even the biggest pessimists in the world will claim to be "realists." And it's true, that IS reality for them. It doesn't have to be reality for you.

Your job is to focus on yourself and your life. You don't have to prove anything to anyone or convince anyone of this. If they see the great big positive changes in your life, they will ask you what your secret is, and then you can tell them.

Every morning, and every night, take a few moments to reaffirm your super positive beliefs:

The world is a loving place.
People are all good inside.
You are worthy of everything great in the world.
Life is fun.
Life is an adventure.
Great things happen for you.

Though if you look at yesterday, or last week, or last year, you may be able to pick out "proof" that these things are not true, remember, that's just because your inner beliefs were not these things at the time.

Keep strong to these beliefs, and let your intuition be your guide. If something feels positive, or exciting, or just plain good, go with it. Your mind may tell you that things are too good to be true, or that you're being naïve or foolish, but that's just because it developed those habits and that is what's familiar.

Are you building a life based on love, or based on fear?

In relationships, do you act because you fear being alone, or fear there is no one better for you, or truly because you love the person you are with?

In work, do you love your work? Do you feel you are able to express yourself, and freely contribute? Do you feel that you are valued? Or, are you only there because you fear bills at the end of the month, or fear that there are no other jobs or work for you that you may like more and where they may value you more?

A life built on actions of fear will never feel secure. Worry lives here. When something ends or someone leaves, it will feel like an enormous loss and will be difficult to let go.

A life built on love will always feel secure. Knowing you are important and deserving of love and appreciation means that even if someone leaves, or you are fired, you know that there is someone or something better in store for you. You will be able to let things go freely, and not try to win back or chase people who don't love or appreciate you.

We've all heard that our minds are like computers.

Our computer minds were programmed in childhood by our parents. You wouldn't tell an older computer that it needs to "just get over" it's faulty programming, but many people tell themselves and eachother to "just get over" their childhood.

Programming repeats until it is changed, and not one second before.

You can't just get over it.

You need to open up the computer and find what programming is incorrect, then reprogram it. Incorrect programing is fear based, whereas correct programming is love based.

How do you recognize faulty programming?

Just look around. We go to what is familiar. We marry people like our mothers and work for people like our fathers. Current friends may be like our siblings.

While we cannot go back and change our childhood, we can change our life in the present.

We can realize what we've just accepted because it's familiar, not because it was good for us, and learn to recognize it in our current relationships.

We can then reprogram our computers. Reprogram what we believe about ourselves, let go of fears, doubts, worries, and base our new programming in love, confidence, and self-worth instead.

From there, our relationships and careers will begin to change immediately for the better.

The other people may change, or they may disappear from our lives.

What they choose to do is not up to us.

The only thing that is up to us is what we welcome or do not allow in our lives anymore.

Recipe for Positive Change

1. Decide what you want
2. Think about all the reasons why it can't happen
3. Worry
4. Try to just live with a life that's "fine"
5. Worry some more
6. Listen to anyone who tells you it's impossible
7. Be OK with giving up things that you don't really love
8. Know you can do it
9. Go for it
10. Achieve it!

***Note: if you skip steps 2-6, you can save a whole lot of years of preparation time!

The Keys to Happiness

The question is often asked, "What are the keys to happiness?" The answers vary, but mainly lie in the enjoyment of life and accepting what "is."

Well, what on earth does that mean?

If you receive a new sweater, enjoy the softness and warmth of it. When it gets old and holey, or if you forget it on the train, don't be sad about what used to be.

When a person comes into your life, enjoy their company, enjoy every moment spent with them. If they go away, or if they pass away, don't spend the rest of your life mourning their "loss." The only thing that exists is this moment. The past is a story which no longer exists but sometimes keeps people chained to wonderful or awful memories of it, and the future does not exist yet and no matter how much a person worries or looks forward to it, it rarely turns out exactly the way they thought it would.

Imagine if the world were to end every night and begin every morning. You'd have no regrets to hold onto and would make certain to make every day count. We all know we're going to die, yet we hold onto negative experiences that no longer exist, relationships that make us feel awful inside, and anxiety over things that may never be.

We ought to just focus on this present moment and realize how fortunate we are...we have SO much compared to many places in the world, we have SO much compared to many other times in the world. There is no world war. During the early 1940s, the entire world just wished for the world war to end. As soon as it did, the world sighed. The world should keep on sighing, especially the parts that aren't being bombed.

If you were a King in the 1300s, you lived in a smelly, drafty castle and you could die from the common cold. You live now better than Kings did a few hundred years ago! You have lights, heat, refrigeration, and a toilet that flushes!

If you spoke your mind, especially as a woman, in many places or times other than here and now, you'd be killed. We are free to think and speak about our opinions, no matter how genius or ridiculous they are, and that freedom is guaranteed by our Constitution in the USA. Amazing!

We have cars, roads, we can travel by plane in a few hours to places that even 200 years ago took several months one way! We live in a time of luxury beyond the wildest imaginations of 99.9% of all those who have ever existed.

We have so much to be grateful for, and we'd be so much happier if we realized this every single day of our lives.

Take a day, and every single thing you touch, pretend like it's brand new and you've never had one like it before. Pretend you're a lady or a fellow from the year 1682 who's been transplanted here just now. Nice smelling soap in the shower, comfortable clothing that fits well, an automobile, a job, a fridge full of food from all over the world! These are all wonderful gifts!

Every person you see this day, pretend like it's the last time you will ever see them (because one day...it will be). Give them a compliment that you really mean, even if you've said it before. Most people regret not being able to tell people who pass away how they felt about them, or not appreciating them enough. This is easily cured by doing it every single day!

Now at the end of this day, if you've done it faithfully, you will see how incredibly fortunate you are. You will see all of the incredible things and people in your life.

This, my friend, is HOW to live. This is HOW to be happy.

The KEY is you. The trick is to remember to do it not for just one day, but for every single day that you live.

When you're not happy,
it's Time for Change.

You can only change yourself. If you wait on someone else to change, you're placing your happiness in someone else's hands, based on a decision they may or may not make, sometime in the future.

If you're unhappy with a person or circumstance, you can:

1. Change your surroundings, remove yourself partially or completely.

2. Change the way you look at your surroundings, accept and appreciate instead of trying to change someone or criticizing them.

The Treasure Within

Some relationships shine a bright light into the treasures of our souls. When in love, little things in life don't bring us down, and we feel we can do more, accomplish more, be more. If those type of relationships change or end, we may feel lost without the love from that person.

What's important to realize, is that they were never the actual treasures which made us better, they were only shining a light on the treasures we already are.

Find your own light, and you can always be that positive, happy, loving person.

When you find it within yourself, no one can take it away.

Depression-busting Meditation

Do you ever get into a funky mood? Maybe just one too many unlucky or bad things happen in a short amount of time and it just gets to you? Well, before that bad mood grows, try this walking meditation to lift your mood:

A walking meditation is different than one where you sit, kneel, or lie down with your eyes closed. In a walking meditation, you're fully awake, but you're consciously changing your thoughts and being aware of every moment.

When a few things go wrong, it's easy to get into a thought loop of what an inconvenience this or that is, or how much is it going to cost to fix this...but like the Seventh Law of Karma States, "You can't think of two things at the same time." This is the Law of Direction and Motives. For those who believe in the Law of Attraction, what you focus on increases, so by focusing on something being bad, more bad will soon come.

Instead, walk around your home, and actively look at everything in it. Start the thoughts, "I love my..." and as you look at everything, whether it be your child, your dog, a book you liked on a shelf, your refrigerator, just keep repeating "I love my..." and go around and do a mental inventory.

Pretty soon, you'll see that you have a lot of love in your home, you have a lot of conveniences, and you have a lot of great things. You'll likely FEEL your energy and mood shift from a depressed one into an uplifted one in just a few minutes.

It may sound too simple to actually work, but it really does!

At the end of this walking meditation, make sure to include "I love myself...for being able to see the positive in any situation." Close your meditation with that, and enjoy the feeling of gratitude which lives inside you.

Whatever problems, things that broke, whatnot, there are, you'll either fix them or make do without them for awhile.

You'll get through it.

Whether you're angry or sad about it, or choose to focus on all the good in your life instead and keep your happiness alive is really just a choice.

Find this place inside yourself.

Whenever chaos, strife, negativity or stress get to be too much in the outside world, return here by closing your eyes, and breathing slowly and deeply, picturing this place in your mind.

Imagine this space...warm sunlight and fresh, summer air, and a soft breeze that gently touches your skin.

This is the place of inner peace, not a thought in the world, Visit anytime to feel calm, stillness, centered, happiness.

Life is just a bowl of cherries...

As the saying goes, life really is just a bowl full of cherries; lots of amazing and loving experiences, and also some pits...challenges and learning experiences.

We know there are pits.

But to live in the past, reliving the pits, or to totally focus on the pits in the present, worry about pits in the future, all the while ignoring the great things, would be like eating a bowl of cherries, and the whole time saying,

"There's a pit. There's a pit. There's yet another pit. That last pit was sure a pit. I'll bet there will be another pit soon. Yep. There's a pit. There's a pit..."

That sure would take the fun out of it!

Keep the fun in life.

Keep your focus on the cherries.

Deal with the pits as they come, forget about past pits, and don't ruin the present by worrying about future pits.

Are you an Anchor, or are you Wings? Who surrounds you today?

Anchors hold others down.
They make fun of their dreams,
insult, criticize, belittle, and make
life tougher just by being themselves.

Wings lift others up.
The encourage their dreams,
compliment, accept, inspire, and make
life easier just by being themselves.

All your life, as much as you can, you should be wings for others, and surround yourself with wings. Your spouse, best friends, coworkers, boss, employees, anyone you speak to daily, influences your life, and you influence theirs.

Depending on who is affecting you daily, you can either be held back more than if you were alone, or you can reach heights that you never even could have dreamed of because of their support. Any award winner, movie star, musician, or politician, on the podium, before they get into their acceptance speech, they always begin by thanking those who helped make it all possible, those who they couldn't have done it without... they thank their wings.

Do some people just push your buttons?

Thank them!

If someone is pushing your buttons, it means there is a button to push. Think about why what they said or did bothered you so much, and then you can eliminate that within yourself.

If someone insults you, you can only feel insulted if somewhere inside, you believe it's true. If you feel slighted, someone else got more praise or attention than you for a job or an effort. Were you only making that effort for appreciation, or were you genuinely just doing your best?

Removing your buttons will stop their effect not only from that one person, but from anyone who tries to push them in the future.

They just won't be there to push!

Don't Allow Molehills to Grow into Mountains.

Most people like to be non-confrontational. BUT if someone else already started a confrontation, it's up to you to resolve it, or to let it slide.

Not doing or saying anything is actually a choice itself, and that choice says,

"It's OK, feel free to do it again."

Now, if there's a conflict, and you get a little feeling that you don't like it, the answer isn't to just rile off and make a big deal of it. The answer is to think...

"This doesn't bother me much now, and I don't like to sweat the small stuff, but IF this happens 1000 more times, will it REALLY bother me?"

If the answer is yes, then you need to address it and resolve it now rather than later. If you wait until later, the person will continue to do it because they have no idea it bothers you...otherwise they wouldn't have done it in the first place. If you wait until a year from now, after it's happened another 1000 times, you will have built up 1000 times more energy, anger or frustration, and at that point, it won't be possible for them to resolve it so easily. They won't be able to go back in time and undo the other 999 times.

IF you value the relationship, AND you believe the other person didn't and wouldn't intentionally do something to hurt you, you'll address the little problems as they come up, as soon as they come up, or risk doing permanent damage to your relationship. Give people the benefit of thedoubt that they aren't aware that something they do or say bothers you, and that's why they do it. By making them aware that it's a little deal now, and you will be making sure it will be resolved, and won't BECOME a big deal later.

What's holding you back from receiving everything your heart desires?

No more feeling like you don't deserve them: You do.

No more second guessing: Trust that the world is a great place.

No more pushing great people and things away because you're afraid one day you may lose them: Time is not guaranteed for anyone or anything. We need to appreciate everything and everyone as best we can while they are here in our lives.

Allow great things to come into your life, and they will do so more often.

Mindscrubbing

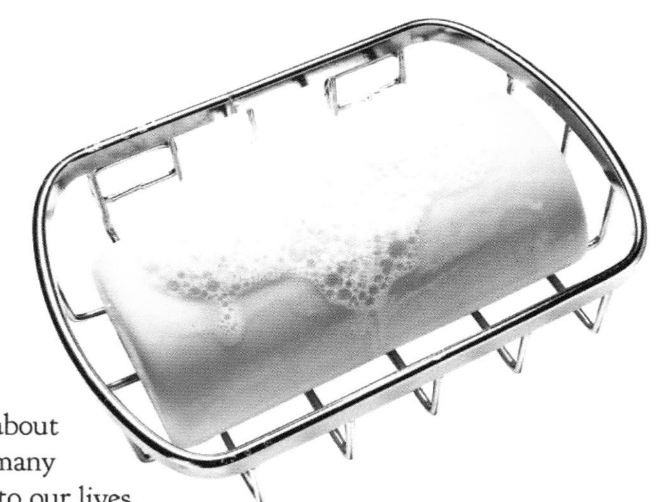

Sometimes people get a little down on themselves when they read an article or book and think, "Gosh, I knew this, but I keep forgetting."

Well, just reading something or learning something once really doesn't mean that you were supposed to immediately get it 100% and apply it to your life right away. In fact, it would be almost impossible to do so.

We're all made up of habits, which are things we've thought about or were taught, then we thought about them or were taught many more times before we really got them 100% and applied them to our lives.

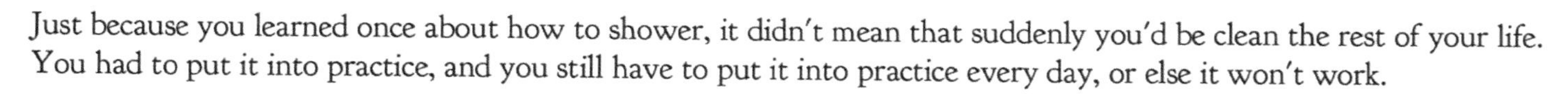

Just because you learned once about how to shower, it didn't mean that suddenly you'd be clean the rest of your life. You had to put it into practice, and you still have to put it into practice every day, or else it won't work.

Just because you learned how to vaccuum, or wash the floors once, it doesn't mean that they will remain clean forever and ever. You had to put that knowledge into practice every few days, and even after knowing how to do those things well, you still have to actually do them for them to have a positive affect.

So what is Mindscrubbing? Mindscrubbing is a term made up to mean doing those same things but for your mind. Our hearts are pure. They always were, and always will be.

It's our minds that can get dirtied up. Whether it's from mean words by others, awful images and stories in the news, on tv shows and movies, or things we learned in childhood that we carried with us unknowingly into adulthood and tell ourselves silently every day.

The cure for all these is Mindscrubbing.

1. Each and every day, start by cleaning your mind while you brush your teeth. Have The Optimist Creed by Christian D. Larson, or some other positive sayings or prayers posted by the mirror.

2. Log on to Facebook and get a little dose of positivity from one of the hundreds of pages dedicated to sharing inspiring messages

3. Think about what these messages mean to you. Keep them in your awareness throughout the day.

4. The more you do this, the more you will remember them when life's little situations present themselves. Before reacting, you may think about one of the quotes you read, and respond in a more peaceful manner.

5. Anytime you feel negative thoughts making their way into your mind, reread quotes, pages, affirmations, or books that you know contain a lot of wisdom and inspiration. There are free videos on Youtube as well.

6. Avoid engaging in or even listening to negative words. Gossip, complaints, arguments...most of the time they only end up making you feel depressed, and don't really accomplish anything. Even being a shoulder to lean on for a friend too often... it's a kind and helpful thing to do, but make sure to make time for positive conversations as well. Positive conversations help both you and the other person to stay happy.

7. At night before you go to sleep, think of all the things you have in life to be grateful for. This will calm the mind and allow for restful sleep and good dreams :)

Repeat daily for best results.

A lot of times, we wish we had some more support.

Encouragement, help, kind words, they are all great to have, but they are not the most important thing.

The most important thing is that you 100% believe in yourself.

Once you do, others will, too.

If the entire world believed in you, but you didn't, you would not be able to accomplish a thing.

Stay focused on your feelings, your goals, know that you are able, and do what you can everyday toward making your dreams become real and true.

Soon, you will start to see magic happen all around you.

Perserverance

When you trust, believe, hope, pray, and try all that you can, it may seem like all that effort is getting you...nowhere.

Be the Gold Prospector.

He patiently focuses on the task
at hand, sitting through cold water
and a heck of a lot of dirt.

He stays because he knows
there is gold to be found.

A lot of other prospectors quit.
Well, the second they quit trying,
they're never going to find
any gold, that's for sure.

It may take days, it may take weeks,
it may even take years, but all he needs
to find is one little gold nugget,
and all his efforts become worthwhile.

Be the prospector.

Keep believing, trusting, hoping, praying, trying,
and doing what you can, and know that one day,

your little nugget will show up and make it all worthwhile.

The road may be long, but the views along the way are spectacular.

Take it all in, and enjoy each moment.

Be grateful for every experience...even the bumps in the road.

By the time you get to the end, you'll see why they were there. Even though at times they were very painful, they led to other things which led to even greater things that would not have been possible without them.

Looking back, you'll realize the trip was well worth it.. ...bumps and all,

and you'd do it all again if you could.

Life

1. The purpose of life is to love
2. The meaning of life is compassion
3. The point of life is to learn these things.

1. Love involves you and the entire Universe, here and hereafter.

2. Compassion towards all. Compassion towards enemies allows you to see that they never really were enemies at all. They were just people acting out of fear, ignorance, lack of self-esteem, or a mix of the three.

3. Learning cannot effectively be done through words. The lessons must be discovered and felt firsthand. Don't pity the poor and downtrodden, or those who struggled to overcome. If you must, pity those who were always wealthy, sheltered, loved, and protected. For they are the ones who will live and end their lives never fully knowing what it was all about.

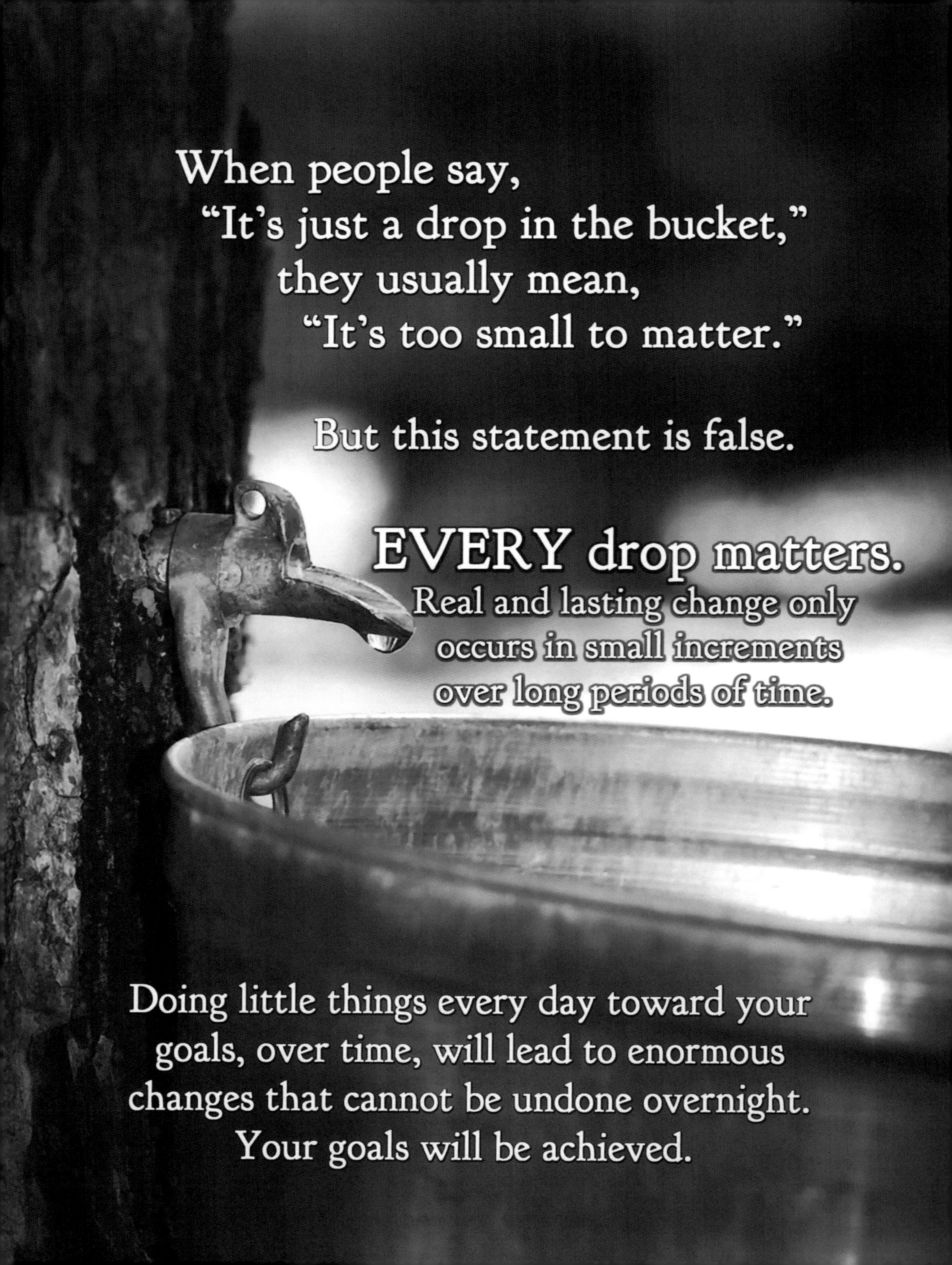

When people say,
"It's just a drop in the bucket,"
they usually mean,
"It's too small to matter."

But this statement is false.

EVERY drop matters.

Real and lasting change only occurs in small increments over long periods of time.

Doing little things every day toward your goals, over time, will lead to enormous changes that cannot be undone overnight. Your goals will be achieved.

What's the point of goals?

Well, whenever you want to go somewhere in your car, you

1. Decide where you want to go
2. Figure out how to get there
3. Get in your car and go

There may be construction, or traffic, or rain or snow, but you know that you're heading in the right direction, so you keep on going. Sooner or later than you first thought, you get there!

The same is true for life. In your health, relationships, career or job, decide if you're happy or not. If not, then,

1. Decide what you would like things to look like instead
2. Research things on google, talk to friends who have more of what you'd like, read books by people who've achieved these goals....get an idea of what you'd need to do to make it happen.
3. Do it! Move in the direction of your goals. Do something, anything, every single day.

You may encounter setbacks, you may find a lot of people want to do the same things, and some days you may feel like just giving up. But keep going!

KNOW that sooner or later, eventually, you'll get there, and you will.

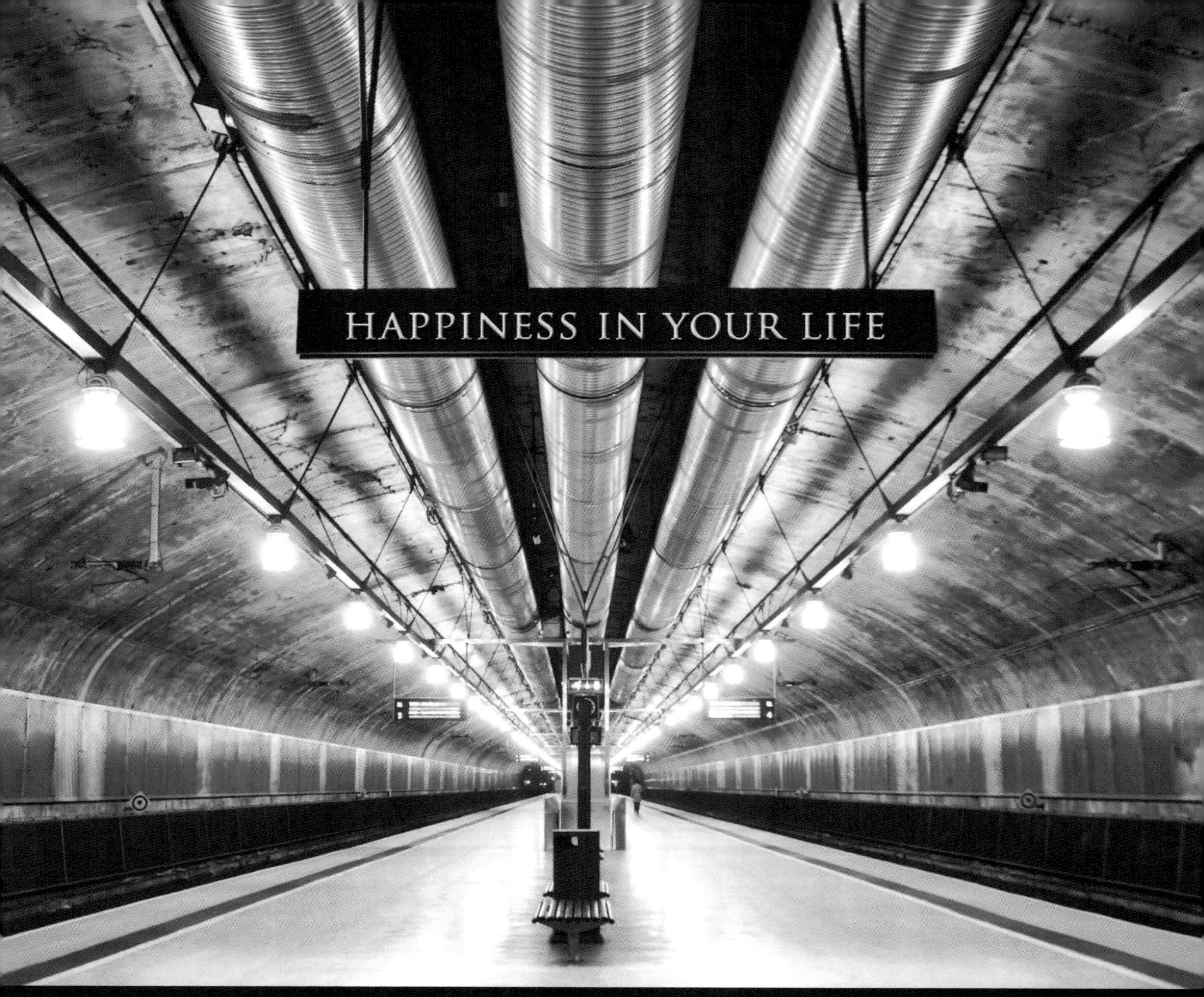

OPPORTUNITIES ARE LIKE SUBWAY CARS
AND YOUR LIFE IS LIKE THE STATION.

ONE THAT'S BEEN MISSED IS PAST AND GONE

BUT THERE WILL BE ANOTHER ONE COMING VERY SOON

DON'T KEEP LOOKING IN THE DIRECTION
OF THE ONE THAT'S GONE
OR YOU'LL MISS THE NEXT ONE....
AND THE NEXT ONE...AND THE NEXT ONE...

The Princess and The Dragon

Tired of waiting for a Prince to come and save her, the Princess summoned up all her courage, grabbed a sword, and went to slay the dragon or demand that he set her free immediately.

"I'm not afraid of you anymore!" she shouted, though trembling inside.

"Madame, there's no need for violence, really. I never said you had to stay, although I have wondered why you had for so long." The Dragon said, terrified.

"Oh. Well, OK then," said the Princess, a little embarrassed.

As she walked away from the Dragon's Lair, she realized a few things...

The only things that ever truly imprisoned her were her false fears, and waiting for someone to come along and save her, when all along she could have saved herself.

Don't be a prisoner to your fears.

This is your life.

Own it.

Have the courage to stand tall and do what makes you happy!

Misery loves company,

But you get to choose how you will R.S.V.P.!

Why waste time complaining about things you can't change, getting upset, sad, or angry for no reason?

Time is much better spent with positive people, talking about great things, or even hopeful futures for things that aren't so great right now.

Stay away from the pity party, it will only bring you down!

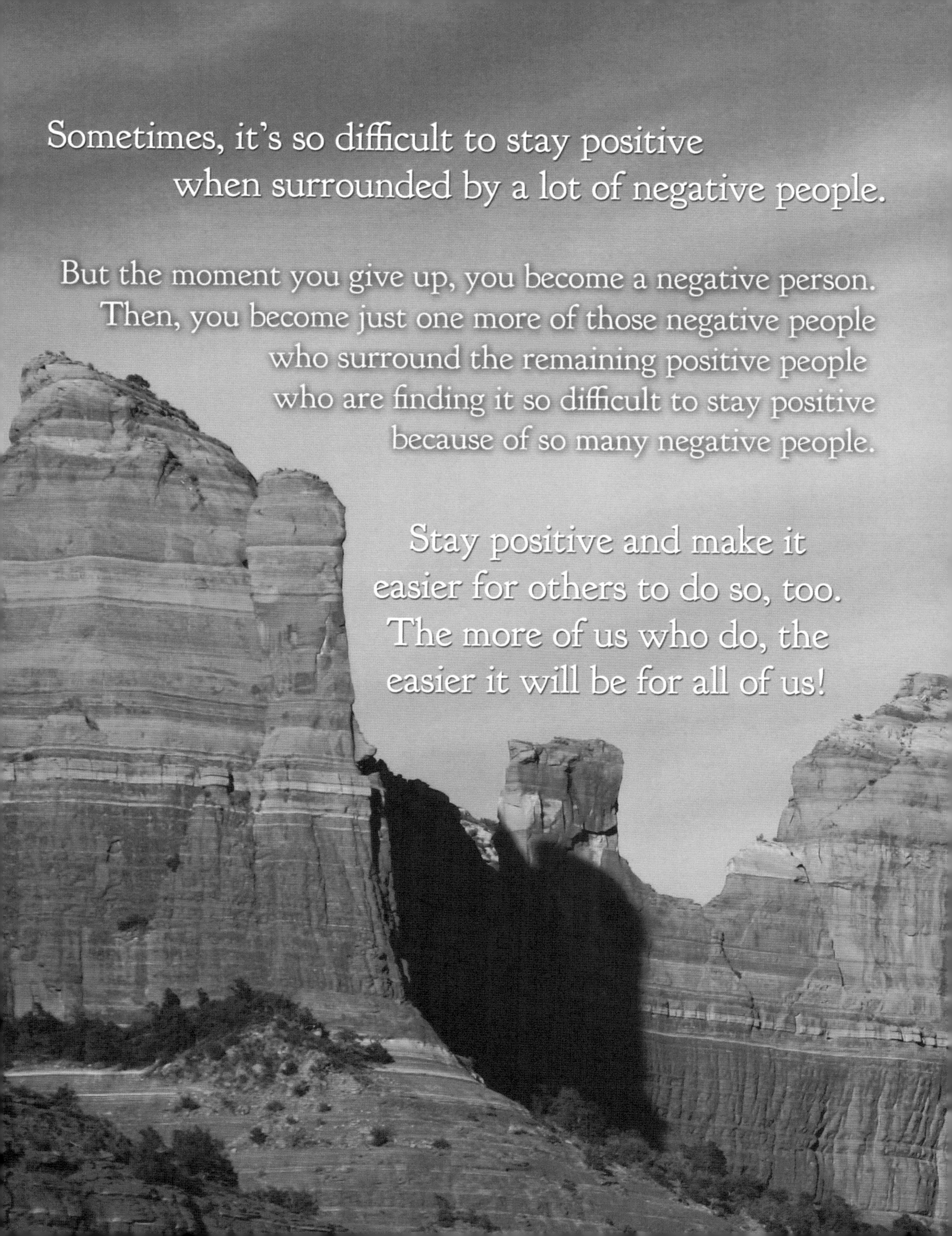
Sometimes, it's so difficult to stay positive
when surrounded by a lot of negative people.
But the moment you give up, you become a negative person.
Then, you become just one more of those negative people
who surround the remaining positive people
who are finding it so difficult to stay positive
because of so many negative people.
Stay positive and make it
easier for others to do so, too.
The more of us who do, the
easier it will be for all of us!

How many psychics do you know?

Well then, quit expecting that anyone "should just know" anything!

Tell people what you need, what upsets you, or what you wish they would keep in mind. If someone isn't acting considerate towards you, maybe they're totally unaware of it and truly just don't know, but would change immediately if they did.

They may be oblivious to what you see as obvious!

Give them the benefit of the doubt and tell them, even if it's a little uncomfortable to ask anyone for anything. You're not complaining. If you were unintentionally upsetting anyone, you would want them to let you know, too, right?

It can't be fixed if they don't even know it's broken!

If the Sun could talk,
it would never say,

"That's it, I give up.
I quit. Nobody cares."

It would always say,
"Well, I did the best I could today. I showed up early,
shone as bright as I could all day, then went in for the night.
That's all I can do, and that's all I will do, every single day."

Maybe we should all try to be
a little more like the Sun?

Show up in life.
Do your best every day.
Try to remain positive.
Rest.
Repeat.

Every person from your past
lives as a shadow in your mind.
Good or bad, they all helped you
write the story of your life, and
shaped the person you are today.

One of the keys to a happy life is balance.

Especially at the turn of decades, 30, 40, 50 years old,
we reflect on how we have spent our time...

If we worked most of the decade, we think we should
have vacationed more, traveled, spent time with family and friends.

If we spent most of the decade traveling, vacationing, and
spending time with family and friends, we tend to feel like
we have not accomplished enough toward personal goals.

To enjoy life means to find the right blend of work and play,
solitude and social life.

Sleep and wakefulness are a daily reminder to balance.
Too much sleep and we feel like we've missed out on most of the day,
and too little sleep and we feel a deep need to rest.

Like the ebb and flow of the tides, balance is a natural part of life.

When passing through the storms of life,
please remember:

1. It could be worse
2. It will get better.

Stay strong, focus on what you can do,
not what you cannot, and know that
the clouds will soon part,
and the sun will return again.

Start with some ordinary sand.
Heat it, put it through some trials, and it becomes glass.
Glass can look nice and shiny, but only having
been through one trial, it is easily shattered. It was not very strong.

But if you take that sand, heat it more, crush it, compress it, put it
through this over and over for years and years, much of it disintegrates.
That which did not disintegrate became a diamond. It became stronger,
more resilient, with a depth, clarity, and beauty to it that cannot
be matched. It cannot be shattered with just one blow.

If you have been through many trials,
if you have been heated, crushed, pressured, and driven
to your very limit, you may feel as though you cannot take anymore.
But realize, please realize, you are stronger, more resilient, more
beautiful, and have more clarity and depth than ever before.
You can no longer be shattered with just one blow.

If you have made it through, you are precious and rare.

You are, indeed, a diamond.

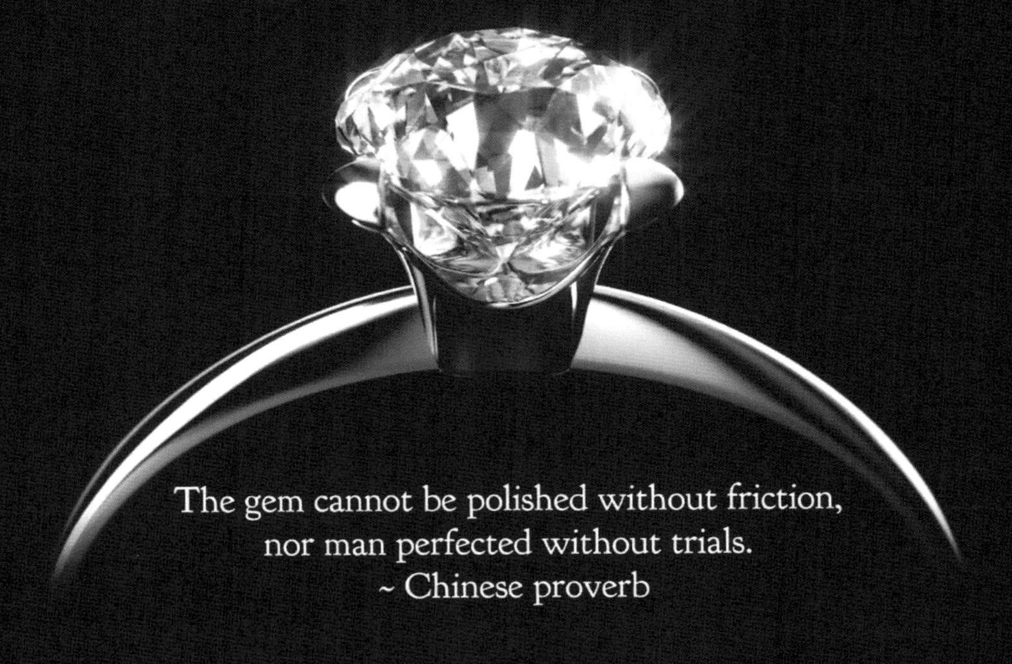

The gem cannot be polished without friction,
nor man perfected without trials.
~ Chinese proverb

7 Steps to Happiness:

Think Less, Feel More

Frown Less, Smile More

Talk Less, Listen More

Judge Less, Accept More

Watch Less, Do More

Complain Less, Appreciate More

Fear Less, Love More